MAR - - 2016
W9-AYR-399
Woodridge Public Library

The Lost Princess

★ BOOKS IN THIS SERIES ★

Trouble at Trident Academy: Book 1
Battle of the Best Friends: Book 2
A Whale of a Tale: Book 3
Danger in the Deep Blue Sea: Book 4
The Lost Princess: Book 5
The Secret Sea Horse: Book 6
Dream of the Blue Turtle: Book 7
Treasure in Trident City: Book 8

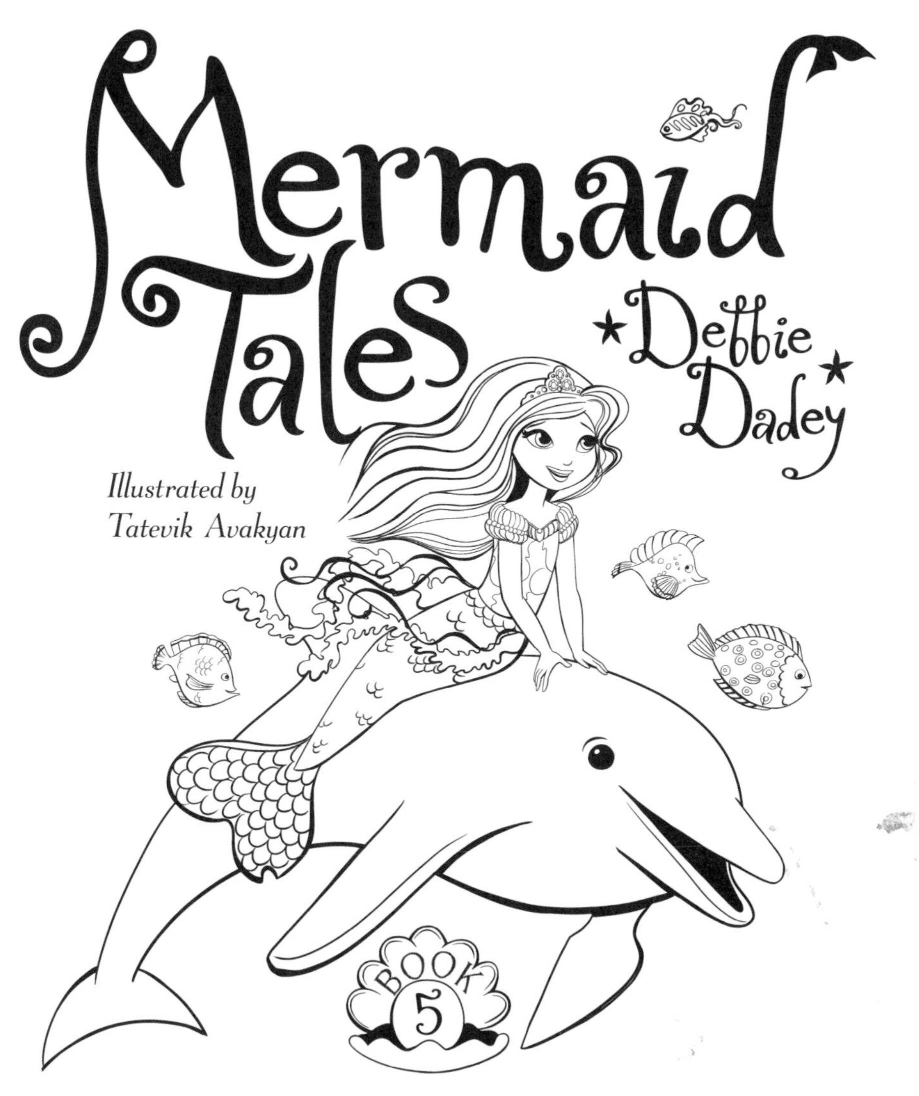

The Lost Princess

ALADDIN

NEW YORK LONDON TORONTO SYDNEY NEW DELHI

WOODRIDGE PUBLIC LIBRARY
3 PLAZA DRIVE
WOODRIDGE, IL 60517-5014
(630) 964-7899

ABDOPUBLISHING.COM

Reinforced library bound edition published in 2015 by Spotlight, a division of ABDO, PO Box 398166, Minneapolis, Minnesota 55439. Spotlight produces high-quality reinforced library bound editions for schools and libraries. Published by agreement with Aladdin.

Printed in the United States of America, North Mankato, Minnesota.
112014
012015

This book is a work of fiction. Any references to historical events, real people, or real locales are used fictitiously. Other names, characters, places, and incidents are the product of the author's imagination, and any resemblance to actual events or locales or persons, living or dead, is entirely coincidental.

ALADDIN
An imprint of Simon & Schuster Children's Publishing Division
1230 Avenue of the Americas, New York, NY 10020
First Aladdin paperback edition May 2013
Text copyright © 2013 by Debbie Dadey
Illustrations copyright © 2013 by Tatevik Avakyan
All rights reserved, including the right of reproduction
in whole or in part in any form.
ALADDIN is a trademark of Simon & Schuster, Inc.,
and related logo is a registered trademark of Simon & Schuster, Inc.

LIBRARY OF CONGRESS CATALOGING-IN-PUBLICATION DATA

This book was previously cataloged with the following information:

Dadey, Debby.
The lost princess / Debby Dadey ; illustrated by Tatevik Avakyan.
p. cm. (Mermaid tales ; bk. 5)
Summary: Shelly is a princess! A real princess! It's been a well-kept secret in Trident City, but now the word is out, and Shelly doesn't know how to act! Should she start wearing a glittery crown? Or move to a grand undersea palace? Will her friends have to call her Your Highness? Being a princess may be exciting, but Shelly's not sure she can truly play this royal part.
1. Schools--Juvenile fiction. 2. Princesses--Juvenile fiction. 3. Mermaids--Juvenile fiction. I. Avakyan, Tatevik, 1983- ill.
[Fic]--dc23
PZ7.D128 Lo 2013
2012950452

978-1-61479-326-7 (reinforced library bound edition)

Spotlight

A Division of ABDO
abdopublishing.com

To the students, faculty, and families of
Sandy Hook Elementary

Acknowledgment

Thanks to Shelly Plumb of Harleysville Books for your support.

N
E
S
W
The Mayor's House
Pearl's Home
Trident School for Languages
Trident City Hall
Big Rock Cafe
Trident Academy
Trident Plaza Hotel
The Coral Reef
56
Reef 56 Hotel
Merlin's
Angel Fish Antiques

Kelp Fields
Echo's House
People Museum * Shelly's Home
Manta Ray Station
Reef's Fish Store
Little V
Whale Mountain
Big V
Trident City

Cast of Characters
Shelly
Echo
Kiki
Pearl
Rocky

Contents

The Lost Princess

Bloodsuckers

"CLASS, HERE'S A RIDDLE. What creature has a head, a soft body, and one foot?" Mrs. Karp asked her classroom of twenty third graders.

One excited merboy blurted out, "A dolphin with a big belly?"

Mrs. Karp raised a green eyebrow. "No, Rocky, these creatures sometimes have a shell. Can anyone else tell me the correct answer?"

Shelly Siren pushed her red hair out of her face and slowly raised her hand. "Is it a mollusk?"

Mrs. Karp slapped her white tail on her marble desk. "Correct! And mollusks are the subject of our next project."

Rocky groaned. "Mrs. Karp, do we have to do *another* seaweed report?" The entire class held its breath. The merkids had been at Trident Academy for only a few weeks, and already they'd done assignments on sharks, whales, krill, and famous merpeople.

"No. Instead of reports we'll be making

sculptures!" Mrs. Karp said. "Tomorrow your art teacher, Miss Haniver, will give you a lesson on sculpting. Won't that be delightful?" Mrs. Karp smiled at the merboys and mergirls.

Shelly thought making a sculpture sounded hard, but she hoped it'd be easier than a written report. She'd much rather be playing Shell Wars than sculpting or writing a paper. Shell Wars was a fun game where you used a whale bone to toss a shell into a chest guarded by an octopus, while the other team tried to stop you from scoring.

Shelly's good friend Kiki Coral asked, "Mrs. Karp, I read in the *Trident City Tide* that there's a group of vampire squid living on the other side of Whale Mountain. Are they mollusks?"

Mrs. Karp nodded. "Yes, they are. Vampire squid are one of my favorite mollusks because their light organs make a lovely glow when they are disturbed."

"Vampire squid?" Rocky gasped. "I've heard about them. They come into your shell at night and suck your blood!"

A few merkids squealed.

Shelly's other close friend, Echo Reef, looked ready to cry. "Is that true?"

Mrs. Karp frowned at Rocky. "Of course not. That's just an old mertale told to scare merkids."

Echo's eyes widened and her pink tail shook. "It worked," she whispered to Shelly. "I'm terrified."

"Now, students, we have quite a busy day. First, we're going to meet Madame Hippocampus, who will teach you merology. Then, after lunch, we'll visit the library so you can decide which mollusk you would like to sculpt."

Rocky and a few other boys frowned. "Do we have to study merology?" Rocky asked.

"Of course," Mrs. Karp said. "To be a well-rounded merperson, you must know everything about merhistory, government, and society. And, class, if you have never seen a hippocampus before, do not scream when you first see Madame. It is not polite."

"A hippocampus!" Rocky shrieked. "I heard they have six heads and twelve eyes!"

Mrs. Karp glared at Rocky. "That will be quite enough. You must stop spreading these silly rumors. They can only cause trouble."

"What's a hippocampus?" Shelly whispered to Kiki as they glided to line up. Kiki was probably one of the smartest merstudents in class and usually knew the answers.

Kiki whispered back, "A hippocampus is part dolphin and part horse. But I've never seen one. I wonder which part is which."

"I guess we'll find out soon enough," Shelly said. "Whatever she looks like, I sure hope she's nice."

Hippocampus

"OH MY NEPTUNE! WHAT IS wrong with Trident City?" Pearl Swamp complained as the third graders floated down the hall to merology class. "We have bloodsuckers around the corner and hippopoopuses for teachers."

"That's 'hippocampus,'" Kiki corrected Pearl.

Pearl rolled her green eyes. "I don't care how you say it, it's still awful. Six heads are horrible!"

Shelly started to tell Pearl that Madame Hippocampus probably didn't have six heads, but they were already by the merology room. In a mersecond Pearl would see for herself.

In spite of Mrs. Karp's warning, several students gasped when they first saw Madame Hippocampus. Even Shelly jumped when she saw the teacher's large horse face, hooves, and plump lower end of a dolphin. Shelly figured Madame must be used to that reaction from merkids, because she chuckled. "Welcome to my lair!" she announced with a big smile.

Rocky snickered quietly. "Now, that's a dolphin with a big belly."

"Ah, Master Rocky Ridge," Madame Hippocampus said. "The first to speak is the one I seek! You have volunteered to be my assistant. Please come to the front of the classroom."

Rocky's cheeks turned red as he slowly drifted toward Madame. "You will point to the correct place on this chart as we discuss the merpeople hierarchy," she told Rocky.

"What is a hierarchy?" Shelly asked. Then she immediately put her hand over her mouth. Maybe Madame didn't like people asking questions.

"Shelly Siren, I am glad you, of all mermaids, asked that question," Madame said.

Several merstudents whispered, "How does she know our names already?"

Pearl muttered, "She's creepy. Is she magical?"

Luckily, Madame ignored the muttering. She told the class to find their seats. Then she addressed Shelly's question. "'Hierarchy' is just another word for the levels of rulers of our undersea world. As

you can see from my chart, emperor or empress is the highest royalty, but rarely do we have such a leader.

"All our rulers are born into their positions, except of course for mayors, who are elected. Emperors or empresses are chosen from the kings or queens by a high council, if there is a need."

Shelly scanned the chart. She knew from the lessons her grandfather taught her when she was a small fry that Trident City belonged to the Western Oceans. It was governed by King Rudolph and Queen Edwina. Shelly knew that even brothers and sisters of the kings and queens were royalty, and their children were princes and princesses.

Shelly's grandfather hadn't been strict about much of her education, but he had made sure she was taught everything on the chart. He had made it into a fun mermaid-royal guessing game, so Shelly even knew the location of most royals' castles and estates. She'd never actually seen one, since none of them were near Trident City, but it had been interesting to learn about. Maybe merology class would be easy.

Rocky pointed to the lowest level of the chart. "My dad is the mayor of Trident City," he bragged.

Pearl raised her hand. "My cousin is married to Duke Armas of Vortex," she said. "A duke is higher up on the chart than a mayor."

Emperor and Empress
(only in times of crisis)

King Cid and Queen Beryl of the Southern Oceans

King Knut and Queen Haley of the Northern Oceans

Queen Hoshi of the Eastern Oceans

King Rudolph and Queen Edwina of the Western Oceans

Duke Diego and Duchess Lani

Duke Armas and Duchess Lenore

Duke Ivan and Duchess Michiko

Duke Fulton

Baron Basil and Baroness Amara

Baron Anders and Baroness Inga

Baroness Jena

Baron Garvey and Baroness Erin

Mayor Calida

Mayor Denby

Mayor Keiko

Mayor Ridge

"Yes," Madame Hippocampus agreed, "but a princess is on a higher level than a duke. And, class, we are honored to have one in this very class." Everyone gasped and glanced at each other.

A princess? Shelly looked around the room. Who in the ocean could it be? She hoped it was her good friend Echo. They'd known each other since they were small fry. Echo would be a fantastic princess. She loved wearing glittering plankton bows in her dark curly hair, so she'd adore a princess's jewels.

If it wasn't Echo, Shelly wanted the princess to be her new buddy Kiki. After all, Kiki was from a part of the ocean very far away. Maybe she was princess of the Eastern Oceans.

"Who is it?" Pearl demanded. "Maybe it's me. My father did give me a crown for my birthday one year. Oh, I hope it's me! I would have special royal tutors and my pick of all the jewels in the sea, and the Rays would play music at all my parties!"

Shelly scrunched her nose. She really hoped Pearl wasn't a princess. With her gold tail, blond hair, and pointy nose, Pearl already thought she was better than everyone else. After all, lots of small fry played at being princesses and wearing crowns.

"Why, it's Shelly Siren, of course," Madame Hippocampus said. "I assumed you all knew. Queen Edwina is Shelly's great-aunt."

All eyes turned to Shelly, who felt herself turning every shade of red. *What is Madame saying?* she thought in a panic.

"Shelly!" Pearl screeched. "She can't be a princess!"

"No way!" screamed Rocky.

"Why not?" Echo said. "Shelly would make a wonderful princess."

"She'd make a better bottom sucker," Pearl said. "She'd rather explore the ocean and be friends with a disgusting lizardfish than be a princess."

Shelly didn't like agreeing with know-it-all Pearl, but she knew this time Pearl was right. Shelly couldn't be a princess, and she really *would* rather play with ocean animals than wear a glittery crown.

"There must be some mistake," Shelly said, looking at Madame hopefully. "My grandfather would definitely have told me if I was a princess."

Madame did not nod her head in agreement. She simply continued, teaching them the king and queen of the Northern Oceans.

Shelly looked down at her blue tail. She couldn't listen to the lesson anymore. She kept hearing Madame's words in her head: *Why, it's Shelly Siren, of course*. Her stomach felt funny and her scales shook. Maybe her grandfather had made her learn about royalty because she *was* royalty. Her parents had died when she was young, and she'd never met many of her relatives. Could it be true? Could she *really* be a princess?

Empress!

WHEN IT WAS TIME FOR lunch, Echo, Kiki, and Shelly swam into the cafeteria. Shelly was glad to be surrounded by her closest friends after the big news of the morning.

"I always knew you were special, but

I didn't know you were royalty!" Echo said.

"Look," yelled Rocky, "it's Shelly, princess of Trident Academy!" Every merkid in the cafeteria, from grade three to grade ten, stopped eating and stared at Shelly.

"Shhhh, Rocky," Shelly hissed. "You don't even know if that's true!"

Kiki stopped eating her hagfish jelly sandwich and asked, "What if it's not a mistake? You would make a great ruler. I mean, you could be an empress someday."

"Empress!" Shelly squealed. "Are you kidding?" Immediately, she was sorry that she'd been so loud. Rocky grinned and nudged his friends at the merboys' table.

He made a low bow in Shelly's direction, and all the merboys laughed.

Shelly took a deep breath and gazed at the carvings of merfolk history on the cafeteria walls. She had stared at them every day since she'd started Trident Academy a few weeks ago. Now she looked

at them differently. The famous kings and queens in the carvings could be her uncles and aunts! She couldn't believe it.

"It's all right," Kiki told her, patting her arm.

Echo nodded. "Come on. Let's go ask Mr. Fangtooth to tell us about his days with the Shark Patrol."

"That's a great idea," Shelly said, glad to have something to take her mind off Madame Hippocampus's news and everyone's whispers.

Mr. Fangtooth worked in the Trident Academy cafeteria. He constantly had a grumpy look on his face, and the mergirls always tried to cheer him up, usually without success. Recently, he had saved them from a shark, and they'd found out he was a retired colonel from the Shark Patrol.

"Hi, Mr. Fangtooth," Echo said. "What was it like being in the Shark Patrol?"

Mr. Fangtooth wiped the lunchroom counter off with a black dragonfish. The fish's open mouth scooped up tiny scraps. The fish burped, but Mr. Fangtooth just grunted.

Kiki tried, "Mr. Fangtooth, what was the scariest thing that ever happened to you?"

Mr. Fangtooth looked right at Kiki and snapped, "Working at Trident Academy."

"Gee, that wasn't very nice," Echo said as the girls swam back to their table.

“Why is he always such a grump?”

Kiki tied back her long, straight black hair with a bow and grinned. “I have a plan,” she said, and whispered the idea to her friends.

Echo smiled. "That sounds great. Watch this."

Echo glided over to the service window of the lunchroom, followed by her friends. Mr. Fangtooth frowned at the mergirls. "Mr. Fangtooth," Echo said. "What kind of hair does the ocean have?"

Mr. Fangtooth grunted again.

Echo giggled. "Wavy. Like ocean waves," she said. "Wavy hair, like mine."

Kiki laughed, but Mr. Fangtooth didn't crack even the tiniest smile. "Mr. Fangtooth," Kiki said. "Why are fish so smart?"

When Mr. Fangtooth didn't answer, Kiki gave the punch line: "Fish are smart because they live in schools!"

Shelly couldn't believe it. Mr. Fangtooth

didn't look up from scraping ribbon worms off trays. So Shelly tried the joke she'd heard a few days ago at Shell Wars practice. "Mr. Fangtooth, which fish is the most famous?"

Mr. Fangtooth put a big sign that said CLOSED! in front of the cafeteria window and swam away. "Well, that was rude," Echo said.

Kiki nodded. "I wonder what made him such a meanie."

"Tell us the answer," Echo said to Shelly.

Shelly shook her head. "I don't know what happened to him."

Echo put her right hand on her hip. "No, silly. I mean which fish is the most famous?"

"Oh, that," Shelly said with a giggle. "It's the *star*fish, of course."

Rocky soared over beside Shelly and announced in a loud voice, "I guess Princess Shelly is the most famous fish in our school."

A group of third graders gathered around Shelly, led by Pearl.

“As a princess expert, I know that Shelly won’t be at Trident Academy for long. She’ll be moving to Neptune’s Castle to begin her royal duties,” Pearl said with an air of authority.

“Is that really true?” Pearl’s friend Wanda Slug asked.

“I don’t know! I don’t know anything about this!” Shelly cried, and raced out of the cafeteria. She stopped out in the hall. Her heart was pounding. Pearl had talked about royal duties and moving. Shelly didn’t want to move, and she definitely didn’t want any royal duties. What was she going to do?

Perfect Princess

"I'M SO EMBARRASSED," SHELLY whispered to Echo when they were in the library later that day. "*Everyone* in the lunchroom was talking about me. And saying all kinds of wild things."

"Don't worry," Echo said. "But if it's true, you'll be perfect."

Shelly's heart jumped in her chest. She very much doubted that she'd make a good princess, but Echo continued, "And if it's not true, then you have nothing to worry about."

Kiki tapped Shelly's arm. "You'd better get busy selecting a mollusk; Miss Scylla is looking our way."

The Trident Academy merlibrarian liked everyone to be busy, so Shelly thumbed through a stack of seaweed papers while her friends checked the rock books. She didn't know if she should choose an oyster, a sea slug, or an octopus. An oyster would be easy to sculpt, she thought, but an octopus would be way more fun.

"Let me have that," Rocky said, snatching a seaweed book from the table in front of Shelly. "I want to see what those killer vampire squid look like."

Shelly shook her head. "You know Mrs. Karp said they aren't bloodsuckers."

Rocky opened his mouth to say something, but Miss Scylla looked their way, and he floated off to a table full of merboys.

Shelly was reading about the nautilus when Pearl sat very close to her. A little too close. "Would you like to come to my house after school today?" Pearl asked.

Shelly was so surprised she couldn't talk. Pearl had *never* been nice to her before. She hadn't even invited Shelly to her birthday party. Finally, Shelly asked Pearl, "Why?"

Pearl shrugged her shoulders. "We have

a big library at home, even bigger than this one. I bet you'll find a mollusk to sculpt that no one has ever heard of before."

Shelly looked around the Trident library. It was filled with shell, rock, and seaweed books. Fancy chandeliers with glowing jellyfish lit up the whole space, making the mother-of-pearl ceiling glisten. "I think this library is big enough," she said.

"Sweet seaweed," Pearl said. "Don't you see that I'm trying to be friends with you? After all, a princess should get to know *all* the merpeople in her kingdom."

Kingdom! Shelly couldn't believe she had a kingdom. "I don't even know if I really am a princess. Madame Hippocampus might be wrong."

Pearl sniffed the water. "Madame Hippopoopus is supposed to be a merology expert. I doubt she is wrong."

Shelly shook her head. She didn't even bother correcting Pearl on Madame's name. "I can't come over to your house after school. I have to go straight home and talk to my grandfather about this royalty stuff. He's the only one who can tell me the truth."

Shelly was glad she didn't have Shell Wars practice today. She had lots of questions for her grandfather, and she sure hoped he had lots of answers.

5

Love Letter

THE REST OF THE AFTERNOON passed too slowly. Shelly tapped her tail fin up and down nervously, waiting for the last conch shell to end the school day.

"I'm going home," Shelly said to Echo when it finally sounded. "I have to talk to Grandfather Siren about this princess business right away."

"May I come with you?" Echo asked. "I want to hear all the details about royalty."

Shelly nodded. Together, they swam by the Manta Ray Express Station.

Enormous manta rays were used to take the merpeople of Trident City from place to place. For just a couple of shells, the rays would take you anywhere in the ocean. They even took merfamilies on long trips. The flashing blue-green light of the eyelight fish warned that a manta express was getting ready to leave.

An elderly merwoman pushed past the

mergirls on her way to the station. Shelly noticed something fall as she rushed by. "Excuse me. I think you dropped this!" But the merlady didn't stop; she just floated quickly onto the big ray.

"I guess she didn't want to miss the last ray of the day," Echo said. "What did she drop? Is it a pirate map?"

Shelly laughed. She knew her friend

had always wanted to find a treasure map.

"No, silly. It looks like a letter."

"Let me see," Echo said, pulling the folded seaweed out of Shelly's hand.

"We shouldn't read it," Shelly said. "It's her property."

"But we have to if we're going to find out who she is so we can return it to her," Echo explained.

"All right," Shelly said, and waited while Echo read. "Well, what does it say?" Shelly asked after a minute.

Echo giggled. "You are not going to believe this! It's a letter—a love letter—from Mr. Fangtooth to that lady!"

"No wavy way!" Shelly leaned over Echo's shoulder as they read together.

My dearest Lillian,

My life is not complete without you. I want to spend my life making you happy.

Yours in love,

Mendel Fangtooth

"*Mendel?*" Shelly said.

"'*Yours in love,*'" Echo said. "Isn't that romantic?"

"It's old," Shelly said.

Echo looked up from the seaweed. "What are you talking about? Love isn't old-fashioned."

"I mean the seaweed letter," Shelly explained. "It's very old. Maybe Mr. Fangtooth wrote it when he was young."

"It's still romantic," Echo said. "And we have to get the letter back to that merlady somehow."

The girls watched as the enormous ray flapped its huge wings and silently moved away from the station, carrying five merpeople on its broad back. "I think that merwoman has bumped into me before," Shelly said. "She's almost as grouchy as Mr. Fangtooth."

"I guess they were made for each other," Echo said.

"We can worry about them later. Right now I have to find out the truth from Grandpa," Shelly said, swimming toward home.

Echo nodded and followed her friend into the People Museum. That's where Shelly's grandfather Siren worked. In fact, he ran the museum and was the ocean's chief expert on mankind. Shelly and her grandfather lived in a small apartment above the museum. Echo loved exploring all the people things, but Shelly thought humans and anything to do with them were silly. She'd heard they couldn't even breathe underwater.

The mergirls found Shelly's grandfather in the circular-shapes section creating a display of the weird human items. One had padding and some sort of spokes or wires attached. Another looked like a flattened jellyfish with letters that spelled "volleyball" on it. Shelly wondered briefly what they could be used for. Then she blurted out, "Grandpa, am I a princess?"

Grandfather Siren jumped. "Shelly! Echo! I didn't hear you come in." He put down a round metal object that had three long sticks poking out of one side, and rubbed his chin. He looked at his granddaughter and spoke softly.

"I wondered when this would finally come up. I had hoped you could have a few more years of an everyday, normal life."

Shelly couldn't believe her ears. "You mean it's true, Grandpa? I'm a . . ."

"Princess," Echo finished for her.

"Why didn't you tell me? Why did you keep it a secret?" Shelly demanded. "Don't you think that I should know if I'm some sort of royalty? Are you royalty too? What about my parents?"

Grandfather looked down at his silver tail. "Perhaps I should have told you. I was waiting until the time was right."

Shelly had rarely been this upset. "When was that going to be? Right before they made me empress?"

"Now, Shelly, you are third in line to the Western crown. There's not a lot of chance of you becoming an empress."

"Third in line!" Shelly knew that meant if something happened to two other merpeople, she would be the queen. "I can't believe these rumors are true! I don't want to be royalty. I don't want to be a princess, and I certainly don't want to be your granddaughter!"

Shelly splashed to her room with tears in her eyes. She left Grandfather Siren and Echo floating with their mouths wide open.

Princess Shelly

SHELLY FELL ON HER SEA FAN bed and sobbed. "I can't believe Grandpa kept the truth from me all these years." Shelly's parents had died when she was quite young, and her grandfather had raised her from a small fry. Never in all the lessons he had taught her about royalty had he ever hinted she was a princess. Was she the only one who didn't know? No, if Echo knew, she would have told her the truth. Shelly was sure of that.

Shelly rolled over and stared at the bioluminescent plankton that glowed on the ceiling of her small room. She still had so many unanswered questions. What was she supposed to do, now that she was a princess? Would she have to move out of the People Museum like Pearl said? Could she ever see her friends again? She had a terrible feeling in her stomach. She had always lived in Trident City.

Shelly usually didn't like sparkly things, but the plankton's bright flashes of light were pleasant.

"I guess if I really am a princess, I'll have to get used to lots of glittery things," she told the plankton as she wiped tears from her cheeks.

Shelly sighed and tried to picture herself as royalty. She closed her eyes and imagined a grand undersea castle. Soon she fell asleep and dreamed. Wearing a shiny crown and a glistening dress that shimmered with diamonds and emeralds, she sat in a large pink shell carriage drawn by majestic dolphins, bigger than any she'd ever seen.

The dolphins pulled her along in a parade. She waved to all the merpeople as she passed by. They cheered, "Long live Princess Shelly! Long live Princess Shelly!"

Suddenly one of the merpeople reached out and grabbed her. Shelly screamed and sat straight up in bed. Grandfather Siren floated beside her, his hand on her arm. "I didn't want to wake you," he said, "but, my little shell, I need to explain."

Shelly shook her head. "You already did."

"Well, not the whole story," Grandfather said. "But I promise I never meant to hurt you. The truth is, your mother was a princess, but she wanted to live a normal life. Your father, my son, married into royalty. When they died, I knew someday you would live as a royal. I kept it a secret so that other merchildren wouldn't treat you differently. Very few people in the ocean even know about you."

Shelly remembered how everyone had stared at her in the cafeteria and started saying all kinds of ridiculous things. Especially Pearl and Rocky. Shelly nodded slowly. "I'm sorry about what I said. It's just so hard to believe."

Her grandfather gave her a big hug and said, "I know, but your life will not change right away. It will be some time before you have to learn about your duties. So let's put the princess business aside for now. Before Echo left, she told me your class is studying the amazing mollusk."

"We're supposed to make a sculpture of our favorite," Shelly told him.

"That sounds like fun," Grandfather said. "While we have dinner, how would you like to learn to speak to them?"

Shelly grinned. She loved learning languages. She'd lost count of exactly how many she knew, but so far her favorite had been the humpback whale dialect. "I'd love it!"

Over the next couple of hours, Shelly the princess became Shelly the squid-talker. She almost forgot all about being a princess . . . until she went to bed.

ALL NIGHT LONG SHE TOSSED AND turned. In one dream, her sea fan was full of sharp rubies that jabbed her in the stomach.

In another dream, there was a war and she had to fight Queen Hoshi of the Eastern Oceans. Shelly woke up shouting, "Let's be friends!"

She was relieved to see that she was in

her own room and the plankton still glowed peacefully on her ceiling. Everything was the same, but deep down Shelly knew that everything was different. A tear slid down her cheek because she knew the truth. Nothing would ever be the same again.

7 A Crown

PEARL WAVED HER ARM BACK and forth, almost jumping out of her seat. "Miss Haniver . . . Miss Haniver," she said. "Did you hear that Shelly is a princess?" It was the next day in art class and Miss Haniver was giving them a lesson on sculpting.

Rocky yelled out, "I heard Shelly eats dinner with King Cid every Tuesday and has servants do her homework."

Shelly stared at Rocky. Where had he heard that?

Several merkids looked at Shelly and whispered. Miss Haniver frowned and said, "There are no princesses in here, only artists."

Art was not Shelly's favorite subject, but today she was grateful that Miss Haniver had made Rocky be quiet about royalty. Shelly scrunched her nose at the large piece of stone at the front of the art room and thought about sculpting. "How in the undersea world is anyone supposed to make a mollusk from that rock?" she whispered to Echo.

Echo shrugged her shoulders. Shelly glanced at Kiki. She looked even more worried than Shelly. Rocky didn't seem troubled at all. He raised his hand. "Miss Haniver, when are we going to get knives so we can start carving?"

Kiki gasped, but Miss Haniver shook her head. "I will not be giving third-grade merstudents carving knives," she said.

"But Mrs. Karp said we were going to make sculptures," Rocky complained.

"Indeed," Miss Haniver said, looking over her tiny glasses at Rocky and patting the rock with her green tail fin. "But there are four different techniques in sculpting: carving—"

"Yes!" a boy named Adam cheered. "That sounds awesome."

Miss Haniver glared at Adam, but continued. "Casting, modeling, and assembling. In casting, we pour mud into a mold. In assembling, we put pieces of materials together. We will attempt modeling, where we form clay into the shape we want."

Rocky groaned. "That doesn't sound fun."

"It's very enjoyable," Miss Haniver told the class. "Today we will be using sand to practice, but when you've made your mollusk selection, we'll switch to clay. Now, take some sand from the floor and give it a try."

Shelly scooped a handful of muddy sand from the ocean floor. She liked the way it squished between her fingers. She tried making an octopus. Some of the arms were really fat and some were too skinny. "This is harder than I thought," she said to Kiki.

Kiki nodded. A big blob of sand sat in front of her. "Does this look like a sea slug to you?"

Shelly didn't want to hurt Kiki's feelings, but the blob didn't look anything like a sea slug. "Well . . . ," Shelly said.

Kiki sighed and dug her hands back into the sand as Rocky teased, "My vampire squid is sucking my arm off." The whole class turned to see Rocky's hand stuck inside his molded vampire squid.

"Save me!" he yelled.

"Rocky!" Miss Haniver snapped. "That will be quite enough out of you for today." She swam with Rocky to the back of the room for a little conference about proper classroom behavior.

"Sweet seaweed, you shouldn't be getting your hands dirty like that," Pearl said to Shelly.

Shelly looked up in surprise. Pearl had talked to her *twice* in one week. "Why not?" Shelly asked.

"Aren't you a princess?" Pearl asked.

Shelly didn't want to answer, especially since she thought everyone was listening. "Yes, my grandfather told me the truth," she said softly. "My mother was a princess."

"Then put that nasty sand away."

"Why?" Shelly asked.

Pearl rolled her eyes and took a seat next to Shelly. "Because you are a princess, and princesses don't ever get dirty."

"Who says so?" Shelly pushed her red hair out of her face with a muddy hand.

"Everybody knows that," Pearl said.

"Pearl," Miss Haniver said from the back of the room, "get back to sculpting."

"Yes, Miss Haniver," Pearl said sweetly, but she didn't move away from Shelly. "Now that I've found out the truth, I have a gift for you."

"For me?" Shelly said.

Pearl smiled and pulled a sparkling

tiara out of a small bag. "My dad gave this to me for my birthday. You can *borrow* it," Pearl said, "until you get your own."

"I can't wear this," Shelly said.

"Why not?" Pearl said. "After all, you *are* a real princess."

Shelly looked at Pearl. She had shiny blond hair and a glistening white necklace of pearls. Pearl looked like she would make a good princess, but that's not the way it had happened. Shelly took another look at the crown and shrugged. "Okay, I'll give it a try."

Pearl giggled and placed the tiara on Shelly's head. It felt tight and cold. Shelly didn't feel any different inside, but she couldn't help noticing the looks of surprise on Echo's and Kiki's faces.

8

"MerStyle" Princess

"I'VE STUDIED A LOT ABOUT PRINCESSES in *MerStyle* magazines," Pearl told Shelly at lunchtime. "Sit with me and I'll tell you everything you need to know."

Shelly shook her head, being careful not to knock off the crown. "I always sit with Echo and Kiki."

Pearl pulled Shelly to her table. "Don't worry. They won't miss you for just one day. Let me be your mermaid-in-waiting. I'll help you with all your royal decisions."

Immediately Shelly was surrounded by mergirls from all different grades. She couldn't even see Kiki and Echo. Where were they?

"Shelly," Wanda said with a giggle. "Can I have your autograph?"

"Wanda," Shelly said, "we're in the same class together. Why do you want my autograph?"

"Because," Wanda said, "I've never met a real princess before."

Shelly sighed, and for the next few minutes she signed at least twenty pieces of seaweed with her name: *Shelly Siren, princess of the Western Oceans.* It was strange when she wrote it for the first time, but it got easier with each one.

Shelly wondered if Kiki and Echo wanted her autograph too, but when she got a glimpse of them, they were sitting at their usual table with their backs to her.

Finally Pearl held up her hand. "No more autographs today. Our princess needs to eat."

"Thanks," Shelly told Pearl. "My hand was getting so tired. I'll probably have trouble doing my homework after Shell Wars practice."

Pearl frowned. "Trouble, my tail. You are a princess. You don't have to do homework.

And forget Shell Wars, it's too rough a sport."

"What?" Shelly said, trying not to slurp her sea grapes. She loved playing Shell Wars and was lucky to have made the school team.

Pearl shook her head. "No, Shell Wars is not appropriate at all. You have a lot to learn about being royalty. But don't worry. I'll help you. What if I come over to your shell after school?"

Shelly started to say maybe, but then she thought about Pearl's home. It was the biggest, fanciest shell in all of Trident City. For the first time in her life, Shelly was embarrassed by where she lived. She didn't want Pearl to see that she lived in such a small apartment. She wasn't proud of herself and didn't like the feeling, but she couldn't help it. "No, my grandfather and I have royal business to discuss," she lied.

"Oh, of course," Pearl said, looking at her bowl of black-lip oyster and sablefish stew. Shelly was shocked. She had told a lie. She didn't have anything to talk about with her grandfather . . . or did she?

That afternoon, when she swam into the People Museum, her grandfather looked at her with surprise. "I thought you had Shell Wars practice today," he said.

"I'm going to quit the team. It's not very princesslike," Shelly told him. "Grandfather, when will I be moving to Neptune's

Castle? Will you be coming with me?"

"Move? Neptune's Castle?" Grandfather Siren said. "We have lived here nearly all your life."

Shelly looked around the huge museum. She had always liked the massive old ship before, but now it seemed a bit run down. "Do you think it is a good place for royalty to live?"

Grandfather glanced at the tiara on Shelly's head. "So that's what this is all about. I wonder who gave you these ideas."

"I was talking to this girl named Pearl today," Shelly said.

"Is Pearl a friend of yours?" Grandfather asked.

Shelly shook her head. "Well, not exactly.

I mean, she really just started to be my friend."

Grandfather's furry eyebrows went up, and he patted Shelly on the shoulder. "I see. Just remember: With great privilege comes great responsibility," he said.

"What does that mean?"

"It means that you must set a good example. You must show people the right way to behave and not think you are better than anyone else."

"But Pearl says I *am* better," Shelly blurted out without thinking. She put her hand over her mouth. She couldn't believe what she had just said. But then she added, "Everyone at school asked for my autograph, and they wanted me to eat lunch with them and invited me to join their clubs."

"Yes, but what of Echo and Kiki?" Grandfather asked.

Shelly felt guilty about not sitting with them at lunch, but surely they understood that being a princess was hard work.

"Everyone wants to be around important and famous people, even if they don't truly know them," Grandfather said. "But they aren't your real friends. Real friends like you even if you aren't a princess, and they don't care where you live."

Deep down inside, Shelly knew her grandfather was right, but she couldn't admit it. She was so confused.

Grandpa Siren scratched his head. "Some members of royalty assume their royal positions early, but it's not required until you turn twenty-one years of age.

Since you know everything now, I will let you decide what you want to do."

Shelly listened to her grandfather. She didn't want to make any big choices—she was only a third grader! Her head hurt from wearing Pearl's ridiculous tiara, and all she really wanted to do was go to Shell Wars practice. But what if Coach Barnacle told her she wasn't allowed because she was a princess?

"I'm going to the park," Shelly told her grandfather. She raced out of the museum, not sure of what would happen when she got there, but knowing she had to go.

9 The End of the Vampire Squid

SHELLY RACED OVER TO MERPARK, holding Pearl's tiara. When she reached the park, no one was practicing Shell Wars, and the Tail Flippers team wasn't flipping. A huge group of merkids huddled in the middle of the kelp field.

"What's going on?" Shelly asked Kiki. Kiki answered, "All practices were canceled because the teachers had an after-school meeting. But Rocky is saying the vampire squid are going to attack our school. Where does he come up with these wild ideas? I'm afraid of what he might do next."

Shelly squeezed Kiki's hand. "I'm really sorry about lunchtime. I let this princess thing get out of hand."

Kiki smiled. "I understand. You are special—no matter what."

Shelly sighed. She didn't feel special, but she was worried. What was Rocky up to? "Come on, let's go listen."

The two mergirls glided up to the large crowd gathered around Rocky. He said, "We have to get the vampire squid before they get us!"

Shelly couldn't believe her ears when lots of merkids shouted "Yes!" in agreement.

"But they haven't done anything," Shelly argued. "You're spreading rumors, just like those stories about me."

Echo nodded. "That's right. Mrs. Karp said that legend about them being bloodsuckers is just made up."

"Do you want to wait until they bite us and it's too late?" Pearl shrieked.

"Old stories are sometimes true!" Adam shouted out.

Kiki shook her head. "This isn't right.

Rocky, if you bothered to read a seaweed book, you would know that these squid are peaceful."

The other merkids looked at Rocky. "Is that true?" one of them asked.

"Of course not!" Rocky answered. "Let's get them!" he yelled, pumping a fist in the water. "We'll make them sorry they ever came near Trident City!"

Echo grabbed Shelly's arm and whispered, "You have to stop them."

"Me?" Shelly gulped. "Why would they listen to me?"

"You are a princess," Kiki replied desperately. "If you don't stop them, there is no telling what Rocky and his friends might do."

Is this what Grandfather Siren meant by "with great privilege comes great responsibility"? Was it up to her to save the vampire squid? They were part of her kingdom, after all. Shelly nodded. She had to do something, but when she looked up, she realized she was too late. Rocky and his merbuddies were gone!

Mollusk Mucus

HURRY!" ECHO SCREAMED to Shelly. "We have to save them."

"I thought you didn't like vampire squid," Shelly said.

Echo shrugged. "I don't, but it's not right to hurt living creatures just because they are different. And maybe Rocky really did make up the bloodsucking thing."

"Let's go!" Kiki said. The three mergirls swam their fastest. They caught up with Rocky's group on the other side of Whale Mountain, a big underwater hill shaped just like a whale's back. A cluster of the strange vampire squid spread out in front of them. Their puffy bodies were different shades of red, blue, and gray.

"Look how ugly they are," Pearl squealed. Rocky picked up a rock from the ocean floor and got ready to throw it.

Shelly put the tiara back on her head. "Stop!" she said, zooming between Rocky and the squid. "I COMMAND you to stop!"

Rocky was so shocked, he lowered his arm. Shelly peeked at the squid and saw that they were flashing the lights on the tips of their arms. She knew from her mollusk research what would come next if she didn't stop Rocky—they would all be squirted with glowing snot!

Shelly quickly thought of her grandfather's language lesson and tried speaking to the vampire squid in mollusk: *"Please forgive us for coming into your home. We will leave in peace."*

Shelly was relieved when she received an answer. *"All is well. We want no trouble."*

"Thank you," she replied. *"I am Princess Shelly of the Western Oceans."*

"Your name will be remembered. You are

always welcome here." Thankfully, the squid stopped flashing their lights and no one got squirted with squid snot.

Shelly smiled. Maybe she had made friends with the vampire squid. She turned to Rocky and the merkids with him. "You!" she said, pointing her finger at Rocky. Her heart pounded in her chest as she continued. "Your father is the mayor—what would he think? You almost caused a feud between merpeople and mollusks. Do you know how many mollusks there are?"

Rocky didn't answer. Shelly didn't know the exact number, but she knew there were a lot in the ocean. "The mollusks would win! And who knows what would become of Trident City! Now, I want you all to go home and never bother these peaceful vampire squid again. That is an order from Princess Shelly of the Western Oceans!"

None of the other merkids moved, but Rocky dropped the rock he'd been holding. "We were just kidding around," he said. "You don't have to get so huffy!"

"Go!" Shelly snapped. To her surprise, every merkid turned around and floated away, except for Kiki, Pearl, and Echo.

"Wow!" Pearl said with a giggle. "That was awesome."

"I didn't know you could speak mollusk," Kiki said. "Will you teach me?"

Shelly nodded. "Grandfather just taught me." Shelly knew Kiki liked learning languages too.

"You are all-powerful," Pearl said. "You could command them to do anything!"

Shelly shook her head. "No, I just did what needed to be done. We should try to be on friendly terms with all the creatures of the seas." She took off the crown and handed it back to Pearl.

"Did you get your own tiara?" Pearl asked. "I can't wait to see it."

"No, Pearl," Shelly said. "That was just another made-up story. I won't be getting a crown until I'm older. I'm grateful I could help today, but my grandfather is right. I'm going to wait before I take on the responsibilities of a princess."

"You don't really mean that, do you?" Pearl snapped.

Shelly smiled at Echo and Kiki. "I just want to be a normal mergirl and hang out with my real friends."

Shelly held out her arms. Echo and Kiki gave her a big hug.

Pearl rolled her eyes. "Oh my Neptune! You are sillier than a sea squirt!"

Shelly knew better. Maybe one day she'd be ready to be Princess Shelly, but today . . . today she just wanted to be Shelly Siren, regular mermaid.

Class Sculptures

★ ★ ★

Octopus, by Shelly Siren

Nautilus, by Echo Reef

Vampire Squid, by Rocky Ridge

Sea Slug, by Kiki Coral

Clam, by Pearl Swamp

The Mermaid Tales Song

REFRAIN:

Let the water roar 

Deep down we're swimming along

Twirling, swirling, singing the mermaid song.

VERSE 1:

Shelly flips her tail

Racing, diving, chasing a whale

Twirling, swirling, singing the mermaid song.

VERSE 2:

Pearl likes to shine

Oh my Neptune, she looks so fine

Twirling, swirling, singing the mermaid song.

VERSE 3:

Shining Echo flips her tail

Backward and forward without fail

Twirling, swirling, singing the mermaid song.

VERSE 4:

Amazing Kiki

Far from home and floating so free

Twirling, swirling, singing the mermaid song.

Author's Note

WHAT GIRL HAS NOT wanted to be a princess? Actually, I still do want to be a princess! But everyone is different and likes different things. I think that's great. Wouldn't it be a boring world if we were all exactly the same? Yikes! We'd be like a huge school of herring!

Hope you'll keep reading the next few pages to find out some true facts about the ocean creatures mentioned in this story. And remember, you are amazing just the way you are!

Your fellow mermaid fan,
Debbie Dadey

BIOLUMINESCENT PLANKTON: Dinoflagellates are tiny organisms that flash a bright light when disturbed.

BLACK DRAGONFISH: The female dragonfish is four times as big as the male.

BLACK-LIP OYSTER: This oyster can be found in the Gulf of Mexico, the western and eastern Indian Ocean, and the western Pacific.

CLAM: Even brown bears like to eat clams. In

the Alaskan mudflats, bears will dig for the Pacific razor clams buried in the mud.

COMMON SEA FAN: Sea fans can grow large enough to make a comfortable bed for any mermaid!

COMMON SEA SQUIRT: The sea squirt passes several quarts of water per hour through its body. It filters out plankton and leaves the water much cleaner.

CONCH SHELL: The most well-known conch is the queen conch, which has a lovely, large shell.

DOLPHIN: The common dolphin is very active and acrobatic. It can swim twenty-five miles per hour!

EYELIGHT FISH: This small fish has a large light organ under each eye that can be turned on and off using a black membrane like an eyelid.

FRY: Small fish are called fry.

HAGFISH: The hagfish can produce enough slime to fill a bucket in just a few minutes! It has special slime pores on both sides of its body.

HERRING: This fish has a silvery body and forked tail.

HUMPBACK WHALE: Humpback whales grow to be fifty feet long and weigh up to thirty-three tons. They live in every ocean, except in the extreme north and south.

JENNY HANIVERS: Fake mermaids were nicknamed Jenny Hanivers many years ago.

KELP: "Kelp" usually refers to the many kinds of brown seaweed.

LIZARDFISH: This fish loves deep water and has a mouth full of needle-sharp teeth. Even its tongue has teeth!

MANTA RAY: The manta is the biggest ray. It eats plankton and small fish. It is also known as the devil ray. They grow up to twenty-six feet across and can weigh four thousand pounds.

MOLLUSK: This group of marine animals includes oysters, sea slugs, and octopuses.

NAUTILUS: This living fossil uses jet propulsion to swim, forcing water out a tube to move in any direction.

OCTOPUS: The Dumbo octopus likes deep water and eats worms and snails.

OYSTER: The Atlantic thorny oyster has a spiny shell to protect it from predators.

RIBBON WORMS: Most ribbon worms live under rocks.

SABLEFISH: Sablefish live on continental slopes. These are areas where the sea floor slopes.

SEA GRAPES: Sea grapes are a type of seaweed. It anchors to a rock or sand and has round sacs that look very much like grapes.

SEA SLUG: The sea hare, a type of sea slug, releases purple or white ink into the water if someone bothers it.

SEAWEED: Seaweed does not have roots, but can make its own food.

SHARK: Sharks do not have a single bone in their bodies.

VAMPIRE SQUID: This is the only squid that lives its entire life in deep water. If an enemy approaches, it flashes its light organs and ejects glowing mucus.

VORTEX: This is a whirlpool. The Old Sow Whirlpool is one of the biggest in the world.

Debbie Dadey

is the author and coauthor of one hundred and fifty children's books, including the series The Adventures of the Bailey School Kids. A former teacher and librarian, Debbie now lives in Bucks County, Pennsylvania, with her wonderful husband and children. They live about two hours from the ocean and love to go there to look for mermaids. If you see any, let her know at www.debbiedadey.com.

COLLECT THEM ALL!

★ ★ ★ ★ ★ ★ ★ ★ ★ ★

3 1524 00664 1981